The
Curious
Kitten

Pet Rescue Adventures:

Max the Missing Puppy

Ginger the Stray Kitten

Buttons the Runaway Puppy

The Frightened Kitten

Jessie the Lonely Puppy

The Kitten Nobody Wanted

Harry the Homeless Puppy

Lost in the Snow

Leo All Alone

The Brave Kitten

The Secret Puppy

Sky the Unwanted Kitten

Misty the Abandoned Kitten

The Scruffy Puppy

The Lost Puppy

The Missing Kitten

The Secret Kitten

The Rescued Puppy

Sammy the Shy Kitten

The Tiniest Puppy

Alone in the Night

Lost in the Storm

Teddy in Trouble

A Home for Sandy

The Homeless Kitten

The Abandoned Puppy

The Sad Puppy

Also by Holly Webb:

Little Puppy Lost

The
Curious
Kitten

by Holly Webb
Illustrated by Sophy Williams

tiger tales

tiger tales

5 River Road, Suite 128, Wilton, CT 06897
Published in the United States 2018
Originally published in Great Britain 2016
as *The Curious Kitten* by the Little Tiger Group
Text copyright © 2016 Holly Webb
Illustrations copyright © 2016 Sophy Williams
Author photograph copyright © Nigel Bird
ISBN-13: 978-1-68010-421-9
ISBN-10: 1-68010-421-7
Printed in China
STP/1000/0199/0318
10 9 8 7 6 5 4 3 2

For more insight and activities, visit us at www.tigertalesbooks.com

Contents

Chapter One
Back to School 7

Chapter Two
Cleo Goes Exploring 25

Chapter Three
The Missing Kitten 38

Chapter Four
Lost and Alone 53

Chapter Five
A Dangerous Search 71

Chapter Six
Amber's Search Continues 83

Chapter Seven
A Frightening Encounter 97

Chapter Eight
Home at Last 111

For George

Chapter One
Back to School

Amber rolled the jingly cat ball down the length of the hallway and giggled as Cleo flung herself after it, her paws slipping on the wooden floor. She loved the way the kitten took chasing the ball so seriously!

Her mom opened the kitchen door and gasped as she almost tripped over the skidding kitten. "Oh, Cleo! I almost kicked you! Are you all right?"

But Cleo didn't even seem to have noticed. She had finally caught her jingly ball and was rolling over and over with it, growling fierce kitten growls.

"I don't think that ball is coming out alive," Mom commented, smiling. "Amber, did you finish sorting out all your new pencils and things for school? Have you packed them in your backpack?"

Amber nodded. "Everything's ready." She got up, looking worriedly between Mom and Cleo. "Mom, what's going to happen to Cleo while I'm at school?"

"What do you mean, what's going to

happen to her?" Mom looked confused.

"I'm worried she's going to be bored," Amber explained. "She hasn't really been on her own that much, has she?"

Amber's family had gotten Cleo from a local cat shelter at the beginning of summer vacation. Amber had been desperate to get a kitten for long time, and her parents had finally agreed. Mom and Dad and her older sister, Sara, had spent hours sitting with her on the couch, looking at the website. But as soon as Amber had seen the picture of Cleo with her brothers and sisters, Amber had known that she was the one. Amber had never seen such a beautiful cat. Cleo was a really unusual color—mostly orange, but with big, dark patches and huge black ears that looked like she needed to grow into them.

Amber had spent the entire vacation playing with Cleo—it was amazing how many games a kitten could invent to play with just a piece of string. Or a feather. Or even the flowers on Amber's flip-flops. She was going to miss Cleo so much—and she had a feeling Cleo was going to miss her, too. Even though Cleo was officially a family cat, and everyone played with her, Amber was the one who took care of her the most. She loved feeding Cleo and making sure she always had clean water—it made her feel that the kitten was just a little bit more hers.

"She's always had Sara and me at home to play with," Amber went on.

"I see what you mean." Mom gave her a hug. "She'll be fine, Amber. Cats are very independent, you know. And think how much time Cleo spends sleeping! She'll just save up her playtime for when we're all home. Anyway, I'll be around some of the time—you know I only work half days. Cleo can distract me from everything I have to do!"

"I guess so," Amber agreed, a bit doubtfully. Cleo did sleep a lot. She was still small, and she didn't seem to understand the idea of taking things easy. She'd race around until she was exhausted and then collapse in a little furry tortoiseshell heap. Amber loved it when she flopped down with her paws in the air!

She wriggled the ball out from

between Cleo's paws and rolled it back down the hallway again. "I'm worried that she'll be bored and find a way to get around the front of the house. She thinks the front yard must be the most exciting thing ever, just because we won't let her go out there. She almost escaped again yesterday when the mail carrier brought that package."

Her mom made a face. "I honestly don't think we can do much about that. We'll just have to make sure she doesn't slip out. I think the noise of the cars would stop her from heading out toward the street, anyway."

Mom didn't look all that sure, though, and Amber sighed. One of their neighbors had a cat who'd been run over and badly hurt, and she hated to think of anything like that happening to Cleo. She was sure Cleo was very clever, but kittens weren't known for being sensible. If Cleo saw something interesting on the other side of the street, Amber was almost certain she'd chase after it. And it wasn't as if she could train Cleo to look both ways first.

Cleo sniffed curiously at the bags in the hallway. Today felt different. Everyone was rushing around. She ducked behind one of the backpacks as Sara came dashing past and almost stepped on her tail. She crouched there, watching as Amber and Sara ran up and down the stairs, looking for things they'd forgotten. Their mom was standing in the hallway, glancing at her watch.

"Come on, you two! I thought you said you'd gotten everything ready last night! We really do need to go—I have a staff meeting before school."

"I'm here, I'm ready." Amber jumped down the last two steps and looked around for her bag and shoes. "I just wanted to find a picture of Cleo to show my friends. Hardly anyone's seen her yet—only Mandy and Lila when they came over."

"I'm ready, too," Sara said, sighing. "I can't believe we're going back to school—it feels as if summer vacation just started. And everyone says high school means a lot more homework."

Sara's high school wasn't that far from the house, but she usually got a ride with Mom and Amber in the mornings and walked home with her friends.

"I don't think anyone will give you much on the first day," her mom replied. "Come on. Grab your stuff, and let's get in the car."

Cleo opened her mouth in a silent meow of surprise as the bag in front of her disappeared. And then she realized—the front door was open!

"Oh, Cleo, no! Sara, stop her!" Amber called out. She was all mixed up with her PE bag and backpack, and she still only had one shoe on.

Sara crouched down to try and stop the kitten, but Cleo darted expertly around her reaching hands and skipped out onto the doorstep.

Cleo caught the different outdoor smells as she leaped down the step and then darted off to investigate the garbage cans. She'd only managed to get out into the front yard a couple of times, and she wanted to explore.

"Did you get her?" Amber came

hurrying up to her sister.

"No, she was just too fast!" Sara gasped. "I'm sorry! I think she went behind the garbage cans. Here, Cleo! Come on, kitty, kitty!"

Mom sighed. "How does she know when we're in a hurry? Amber, can you catch her? Try not to let her go under the car—it'll take forever to get her back out again."

Amber crouched down beside the garbage cans. The kitten was in the flower bed now, peering out through the pink geraniums.

Cleo gazed up at her with round green eyes. She didn't understand why they made such a big deal about her being *here*, when no one minded if she went through her cat flap into the backyard. She looked around, eyeing the pavement and the street beyond. There were interesting smells out there—more cats and other things, too. But the cars speeding past were so loud that she'd never dared to do more than peek around the edge of the wall. She wanted to, though. She was working up to it.

"There!" Amber reached through the flowers and grabbed her, and Cleo snuggled up against her school sweater. The kitten didn't mind being caught, not really. Especially because Amber always gave her cat treats when she brought her back inside.

Cleo dived out of the cat flap and shook her ears angrily. She didn't like the way it banged behind her—it always made her feel jumpy. She licked at the fur on her white front until she felt calmer and then strolled out onto the patio. The yard was very bright, and there were fat bees buzzing around the lavender bush. She could even hear a bird rustling in the apple tree at the far end. But somehow the backyard didn't seem quite as exciting as it usually did.

Cleo sat on the patio, feeling the warm afternoon sun on her fur and wondering what to do. She had slept for a lot of the morning, and now she wanted to play. Amber's mom was working on her computer, and she'd petted Cleo for a bit. But when Cleo had tried to pounce on her keyboard, she'd shooed her away. Cleo was used to playing with Amber, and she missed her. It wasn't as much fun being on her own. She could run across the yard after that bird or wriggle into the lavender and swipe at the bees. But she never seemed to catch anything.... When would Amber come back?

Then her ears flattened and she sprang up, stalking across the patio to the bench by the wall. Amber had gone out the front door. Maybe she was at the front of the house somewhere. If she hopped up onto the bench, she wouldn't be that far from the top of the wall....

Cleo wriggled her bottom and leaped, scrambling from the arm

of the bench into the twiggy mass of
jasmine that was growing up the wall.
She clawed and scratched and pulled
her way up onto the top. Half of her fur
was standing on end, and it was full of
tiny green leaves, but she had done it.
She was almost sure this wall led
around to the front of the house, where
Amber was.

Cleo paced
along the top
of the wall,
then over
the flat
roof of
the garage.
She dropped
back down onto the wall again where
it ran along the side of the little front

yard. She had to pick her way carefully through the tall plants that grew up against it, but eventually she reached the front of the yard, where the wall was lower and half-hidden by bushes. She perched between the bushes, looking out toward the street.

"Cleo!"

The kitten peered curiously around the bushes and saw Amber racing down the street toward her with her backpack bouncing against her shoulders. Cleo stood up and purred, arching her back proudly.

She'd been right! Amber *was* here! Amber would see that she'd been clever and climbed the wall. As Amber ran up to her, Cleo purred even louder and leaned down to rub her head against Amber's shoulder.

"Oh, Cleo," she whispered lovingly, "you're so naughty! How did you get out here? Mom, look!"

"Cleo!" Amber's mom stared at the kitten. "I made absolutely sure she didn't slip past me when I left to get you from school. She was in the house this afternoon—I know she was. She tried to sit on the computer while I was working."

Amber gently scooped the little kitten off the top of the wall. She held Cleo against her shoulder as Mom went to unlock the front door. "But that means she must have gotten around the house by herself," Amber said, looking up at the wall. "She couldn't have.... That wall is too high for her to jump up to, and then she had to get onto the garage roof!"

Cleo looked up at the wall, too, and purred smugly into Amber's ear.

Chapter Two
Cleo Goes Exploring

Now that Cleo had figured out how to climb the wall in the backyard, she was desperate to try it again. Amber had homework to do—which she thought was really unfair on her first day back. She left Cleo gobbling down her snack, hoping she would come and find her when she'd finished. But Cleo had other ideas, and when Amber's dad came home from work, he was met by a purring kitten on the path.

Dad laughed as Cleo danced happily around his feet, and he crouched down to pet her. "You're not supposed to be out here, little miss. Did you slip out? Come on." He opened the front door and called out, "Look who I found!"

Amber and Sara peered over the top of the stairs.

"Oh, no! Was she out front again?" Amber hurried down to scoop Cleo up. "She's definitely learned to climb the wall. Mom said she must have done it earlier, but I thought Cleo might have sneaked out without her noticing. She was on the front wall when I came home!"

"She was only in the front yard." Dad looked at Amber as he hung up his jacket. "I think she'll be okay out there."

"What about the street, though?" Amber sighed worriedly and then laughed as Cleo's head butted into her chin. "Oh, Cleo, are you telling me not to worry?"

"How's Cleo?" Amber's friend Mandy asked in class a couple of days later, spotting the picture that Amber had stuck on the front of her planner. "Has she learned any more tricks?" Amber had told her about all the games she'd invented with Cleo.

Amber rolled her eyes. "Yes! She's learned how to scramble onto the back wall, then climb all the way over the garage roof so she can get into the front yard."

Lila leaned over the table. "Why? What's so exciting about your front yard?"

"Who knows?" Amber sighed. "But it has a street in front of it, that's the problem. There's this really nice lady, Susan, who lives down our street. Her cat got run over last year. He crawled back in through the cat flap with a broken leg. He had to have an operation to put the bone back together with metal pins. Then he had to live in a cat crate for two months to keep him from walking on it."

"But that's not going to happen to Cleo," Lila said comfortingly.

"It could." Amber ran her finger over Cleo's whiskers in the picture— they were so white, and they fanned out like she had a mustache. "She's still little, and she doesn't know what cars are. The people across the street are starting to have an extension built onto their house this week. Mom was telling me. She was saying it might be tricky to get out of our driveway because of all the builders' vans and things. So that's tons more traffic to worry about."

"I'm sure it will be okay...," put in a quiet voice.

Amber looked over at the other side of the table, a little surprised to see that it was Greg who'd said that. She didn't know Greg very well, as he'd always been in the other class until this year. She hadn't seen him on her way to school, either, so she guessed he didn't live very close by. They'd been at the same table for a week now, but Greg hadn't said much at all.

"My mom's cat, Pirate, goes up and down our street, and he does cross the road sometimes. But he's really careful. I bet your kitten will just learn what to do."

"Greg is right," Lila agreed. "Cats are clever. I'm sure Cleo will learn how to cross the street, no problem."

"Maybe," Amber said. She loved how Cleo was so curious—it made her even more fun to play with. But it also meant that she liked to explore everything. She sighed to herself as Mr. Evans told them to stop chatting and settle down. She was probably worrying too much—it was the first time they'd had a pet, after all. She just couldn't shake that little nagging feeling that Cleo was too nosy for her own good.

Cleo sat perched on the front wall, peering out from under a branch and eyeing the men working on the other side of the road. There was one big truck, with a crane lifting huge pallets of bricks. Then there were two smaller vans, and a lot of people going backward and forward between them and the house. She wanted to get closer to see what was going on.

The street was in between her and the action, though, and she didn't like the way the cars roared and growled as they shot past. Yesterday, after a few days of exploring the front yard, she'd actually ventured out onto the pavement. At first she'd just stood by the gate, flinching when a car came past. But they all seemed to stick to the road, and she was sure the pavement looked safe enough.

She'd crept along the bottom of the wall, keeping well away from the street. Then a car had sped by. Cleo had felt the rumbling of the road under her paws and smelled the exhaust, and she'd raced back to the safety of the yard.

She still wasn't quite brave enough to cross the road and investigate the unusual things that were happening on the other side. Cleo edged between two bushes as another van came driving up. But this time when the van stopped, it was on *her* side of the road.

Cleo wriggled out between the thick

stems, her whiskers twitching. The driver was getting out—Cleo could see his heavy boots walking around the side of the van. Then he opened up the back doors and lifted out a box, which he carried across the road to the interesting house on the other side.

Almost without realizing it, Cleo was padding eagerly out into the middle of the pavement. The van was new and exciting, and she wanted to see what was in it.

Then the man was coming back. Cleo ducked under the sprawling fuchsia bush in the yard next door. Amber and Sara always tried to grab her when she went out the front of the house. She didn't want this man to catch her now and stop her from exploring. But the

man didn't even notice her. He just
unloaded another
box and set off
across the
street again,
leaving the
van's back
doors open.

As Cleo
edged out
of the bush,
she came to a sudden halt. Her collar
was caught on the wiry branches. She
pulled at it angrily. She hated collars.
When the safety catch came open,
she tossed her head briskly from side
to side, enjoying the freedom. Then
she hurried out from under the bush,
shaking the dry leaves from her fur.

Cleo sniffed at the tires of the van and then stretched up, putting her front paws on the little back step. The van was full of boxes, some old bags, a folded plastic sheet, and all kinds of fascinating things. There were dark corners

and good smells to investigate, too.

She jumped up, scrambling to get her back legs onto the step, and clambered into the van. It was dusty, which made her sneeze, but that didn't stop her. She prowled further inside and rubbed up against one of the boxes. She liked this place, and she wanted to mark it as hers.

Suddenly, there was a shout from outside and the sound of footsteps approaching. Cleo froze, laying her ears back. What was happening? Was someone coming to chase her out? She backed between the box and a pile of bags and watched, round-eyed, as the doors at the back of the van swung shut with a slam.

She was trapped.

Chapter Three
The Missing Kitten

Amber turned to her mom, smiling in relief. "It's okay! Cleo's not in the front yard. She must have decided to stay around the back today."

Mom nodded. "Maybe the novelty has worn off."

All the same, Amber was a little bit hurt that Cleo didn't come rushing to see her as she stepped into the house. Whenever they'd been out over summer vacation, she'd always come to greet them. As soon as she heard the door bang, she would come dashing downstairs from Amber's room, where she'd been asleep on her bed. Or sometimes she was sitting on the living room windowsill, watching to see them drive up.

The house felt oddly quiet and empty without a little tortoiseshell cat twirling around her feet. "Cleo!" Amber called up the stairs. "Cleo, where are you?"

Mom pushed the front door shut and looked around in surprise. "Isn't she here? She's usually desperate for us to feed her when we get home from school."

"I know...," Amber said. "Cleo! Cleo!" She hurried to the kitchen and out into the backyard. But no kitten came galloping over the grass to meet her. The yard was empty and still, with just a few birds twittering in the trees.

Amber trailed back inside, feeling worried.

Her mom was emptying one of Cleo's pouches of kitten food into her bowl, and she glanced up as Amber came in. She put down the pouch, looking thoughtful. "No sign of her?" she asked.

Amber shook her head.

"That *is* odd. Go and check upstairs, Amber. She might have gotten shut in one of the bedrooms."

Amber smiled. "I didn't think about

that! I hope she hasn't made a mess in Sara's room. Sara got really angry when Cleo tipped over all her hairbands and stuff the other day."

She raced upstairs, but all the bedroom doors were ajar. She checked the linen closet, too, just in case, but she wasn't in there.... Or in Sara's wardrobe, or hers, or Mom and Dad's. She wasn't anywhere at all.

"Mom, I don't know where she can be," Amber said, bursting back into the kitchen. She was trying very hard not to cry. Mom would only say she was getting upset about nothing. But this really didn't feel like nothing. Cleo never missed meals.

Mom put her arm around Amber's shoulders. "Sit down for a minute, have a drink, and let's think about this." She handed Amber a glass of juice and guided her into a chair. "Cleo was around just before lunch when I went into school. And we know she's been getting more adventurous lately, going over the wall into the front yard. She's probably just gone further than before. After all, you've only been back at school a week. Cleo doesn't really know what time you come home, does she? And the fact I'm working different times of day probably confuses her, too."

"I guess so...."

"I bet she'll be back in a minute, yowling if we don't get her food in front of her before the cat flap bangs shut."

Amber tried to laugh, but she couldn't quite manage it.

Cleo stood perched on the pile of old bags, meowing anxiously. She didn't understand why the doors had closed so suddenly. All she knew was that now she couldn't get out. She started to pick her way carefully between the boxes back toward the doors. Maybe when she got closer, she'd find a way to escape. When she pushed on doors in the house, sometimes they opened. Although sometimes they didn't…. She scampered up to the doors and scratched at them with her front paws. They were shut tight.

There was a growling noise and then suddenly the van lurched, and Cleo slipped over sideways with a little squeak of fright. She'd only been in a car a few times, when she was brought home from the shelter and for trips to the vet. She'd always traveled in a cat carrier, padded with a blanket, though. She slid across the floor of the van as it pulled out into the road, meowing frantically. She hadn't meant for this to happen at all.

Cleo pressed herself into a small dark space under a storage locker that had been built for tools. It was a tight fit, but it made her feel safer. Nothing could get at her under here. She squashed herself back against the cold metal of the van's wall and waited.

Eventually the van seemed to slow down, and then it lurched to a stop. The noisy engine was turned off, leaving Cleo's ears buzzing. There was a crunching, clashing sound, and the doors swung open. Cleo wriggled her nose out of the tiny gap and tried to see what was happening. She could smell the fresh air coming in through the open doors, and she desperately wanted to race for them. But there was so much noise. She darted back into her safe hiding place as a huge box slid past her with a shriek of metal on metal and shivered. What if more of the boxes moved as she ran for the doors? She had to try, though.

Cleo laid her ears back close to her head and crept out. With her tummy pressed against the floor of the van, she edged across to the doors.

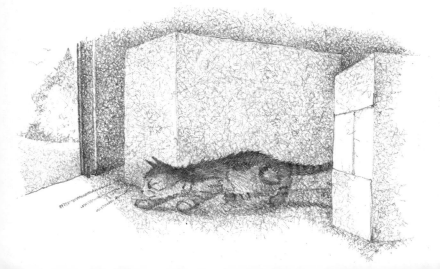

She could see the road outside, and her whiskers twitched with the warm smells of the sunny afternoon. But just as she was getting ready to jump down, the doors clanged shut. She was trapped once more.

Cleo flung herself at the doors with a desperate wail, banging her paws against the hard metal. The doors didn't budge. She should have run for it when she had the chance! Furious and frightened, she stomped back across the van, the fur all along her spine raised, her tail fluffed up. What was going to happen now? What if she never got out?

Miserably aware of how hungry and thirsty and lonely she felt, Cleo meowed as loudly as she could, hoping that Amber would come, the way she always did. *Surely* Amber would come and rescue her....

"Amber, I don't think she has been hit by a car," Mom said gently as Amber's dad came into the kitchen and hung his laptop bag over a chair. "We would have heard. Cleo's microchipped. If she'd been taken to a vet, they would have called my cell phone."

Amber had searched everywhere she could think of. She'd opened every cupboard in the house, remembering the day when Dad had accidentally shut Cleo in the cupboard under the stairs. And then she'd gone back and checked all the drawers, too. When Sara had gotten home from school, the sisters had gone down their street calling for her, while Mom had checked the garage and the shed. But Cleo was nowhere to be found. And what made it even worse was that Amber and Sara had found her collar under one of the bushes in front of the house next door. So now even if someone found her, they wouldn't know the number to call.

"What's up? Has Cleo disappeared?" Dad asked, giving Amber a hug. "She's probably just out exploring."

"Well, that's what I said," Mom sighed. "But it's six o'clock, Dan. She normally has her dinner about four. It's really unusual for her not to show up for that."

"And now we've found her collar," Amber said shakily, pointing to it on the kitchen table. "So we know she was out at the front of the house. What if she's been run over?"

"No, your mom's right. I'm sure someone would have found her and let us know, Amber." Dad frowned thoughtfully. "Maybe she is lost, though. She's still little—she could just have gotten confused about where she was going. How about I take another quick look along the street?"

When Dad came back a while later, he had to admit that he hadn't seen any sign of Cleo, either. As Amber picked at her dinner, she kept thinking of the open cat food pouch, which Mom had folded over and put in the fridge. Cleo must be so hungry, wherever she was.

"Try not to worry, Amber," Mom said as she turned off Amber's light at bedtime. "She'll probably be back in the morning."

"You're not sure...."

Mom sighed. "No, I can't be *absolutely* sure. I really do think she will be, though."

Amber pulled the comforter over her head. She was desperate to sleep so that she could wake up and find Cleo stomping up and down her bed, purring and meowing until Amber got up and fed her breakfast. But she lay awake for what seemed like hours, imagining the kitten hungry or lonely or, worst of all, hurt.

Chapter Four
Lost and Alone

Cleo woke the next morning feeling stiff and cold. She had slept on the pile of bags, but they weren't very comfortable, not compared to her soft basket. She was also desperately hungry. She had never gone for so long without a meal— or without Amber to pet her and play with her.

She sat up, shaking out her paws, and

licked at the fur on her shoulders and neck. She felt so dusty and dirty in here. But washing only made her realize how much she needed a drink of water.

Cleo froze suddenly, with one paw lifted, ready to sweep over her ear— she could hear footsteps. Someone was coming! She ducked behind a large crate and watched eagerly as the van doors swung open. Hands reached into the van, and a box of tools clanked down loudly. Cleo edged forward. She crept around the boxes until she was just by the doors and waited for the footsteps to move further away again. Her heart was racing—this was her chance!

Cleo jumped down onto the street and scurried under the van. She needed to stop and think about what to do next. She had hoped that once she was out of the van she would see her house, the wall around her yard, and maybe even Amber. Although she knew that the van had moved, it had no windows in the back, and she didn't really understand that it had traveled from one place to another. So she was completely confused when she realized that she was somewhere different—somewhere that didn't smell familiar at all. Cleo peered out from around the back wheel of the van, looking up and down the street. She was lost.

Amber waved good-bye to Mom reluctantly and slung her backpack over her shoulder. Lila came running up as she trailed into the playground.

"Are you all right?" Lila said anxiously. "Your eyes are all red. Amber, what's the matter?"

"It's Cleo," Amber sniffed. "She never came home for dinner last night. Mom and Dad said they were sure she'd be back when we got up, but she wasn't!" She swallowed hard. "I didn't want to come to school. I wanted to stay at home and keep looking for her. Mom said she's going to call all the vets this morning. That's in case … in case she's been brought in because something has happened to her."

"Oh, no," Lila whispered. "But you were saying only yesterday that you were worried about her being run over."

"I know!" Amber pressed her hands into her eyes. She didn't want to start crying again, not at school. "That makes it worse," she whispered. "I feel like I made it happen by worrying about it."

Lila put an arm around her shoulders. "Of course you didn't," she said firmly. "All it means is that you were right to worry. And you don't know that anything bad has actually happened! She might just be shut in somebody's garage."

"I guess so," Amber muttered.

Then Mandy came hurrying up, and Amber stared down at her shoes as Lila told her what had happened. She didn't want to hear her friends talking about it—it only made Cleo's disappearance seem more real.

"Did you go looking for her?" Mandy asked.

"Down the entire street. And Dad asked some of the neighbors when he got home last night. If Cleo isn't back by this afternoon, we're going to put posters up."

Lila made a face. "I hate those posters. They're so sad. But I bet they work," she added hurriedly.

"There's the bell." Mandy squeezed

Amber's hand. "Are you going to be okay? Do you want us to say something to Mr. Evans for you?"

Amber shook her head, horrified. Imagine her teacher making it a big deal and the entire class knowing. "I'll be fine. Please don't tell anyone, Mandy. I just don't want to talk about Cleo— it's making me feel too miserable."

After school, Amber dashed out to find her mom, hoping that she'd have good news. But she could tell as soon as she saw Mom on the other side of the playground that she didn't. She looked worried, even though she smiled at Amber and held out her arms for a hug.

"She hasn't come home, has she?" Amber asked, her voice muffled in her mom's jacket.

"Not yet, sweetie."

Amber swallowed. It felt like her heart was swelling up and blocking her throat. "Let's go home," she told Mom, and her voice sounded odd, even to her. "We need to start on the Lost Cat posters. I'll find a good picture of Cleo."

"Yes, I suppose we should," Mom agreed. "I really did think she'd have come back home by now. I wonder if she's shut in somewhere."

"Where?" Amber turned to look at Mom.

"Someone's shed, maybe? You know how nosy Cleo is. If she found one open she'd definitely pop in for a look around. And then maybe the person came back and shut the door without seeing her."

Amber nodded. "Oh, yes! I'll put that on the poster then. We'll ask if people can look in their sheds. And Lila said she could be shut in a garage. I wonder if there's anywhere else...."

As soon as she got home, Amber raced upstairs to find the laptop she shared with Sara. Normally they argued about whose turn it was to have it, but Amber knew that today Sara wouldn't mind if she got it out of her bedroom. She carried it into her own room and started to figure out what the poster should say.

"Amber?"

Amber gazed up at Sara in the doorway. "Look!" she sniffed, holding out the laptop to her big sister. There were tears dripping down her nose.

"Oh…." Sara sat down next to Amber on the bed, peering over at the photo on the screen. "I took that one on Mom's cell phone. Cleo thought the phone was something she could eat—that's why she's so close up. She looks really cute."

"I bet she's really scared, wherever she is," Amber sobbed. "She's not going to understand what's going on, is she? She won't even know we're looking for her."

"I bet she will," Sara said. "She knows we love her, Amber. I'll help you put the posters up, and she'll be home soon. It'll be okay."

Once she'd darted out from under the van onto the pavement, Cleo squirmed under the nearest gate. She still had no idea where she was and why she couldn't find her way home to Amber, but she was so thirsty. She had to find something to drink. She followed her nose down the path at the side of the house and came out into the backyard. She could smell water, she was sure. There was a delicate pattering sound, and she hurried toward it. She was right—there was a huge bowl full of water, with a little fountain in the middle.

Cleo put her paws up on the edge and drank greedily. It tasted odd, not like the water from her bowl at home, but it was still good. She liked the fountain, too, and she darted her head around, trying to catch the drops of water in her mouth. They got on her ears and her whiskers, but she didn't mind— it helped to get rid of the dusty feeling.

Cleo padded across the yard, sniffing for something to eat—she felt much hungrier, now that she wasn't so thirsty. There was a definite smell of at least one other cat around, but none appeared.

Eventually she came to a little tent set up on the grass. She peered around the front flap, sniffing hopefully. There on a rug was a plastic plate, with half a stale sandwich on it. Cleo darted in and gobbled down the sandwich, which was full of dry cheese. It was delicious! She was still hungry, so she washed herself thoroughly all over, making sure she got every last crumb out of her whiskers.

Then she yawned and curled up on the part of the rug that was in the sun.

The yard was quiet and felt safe, and the September sun was very warm. Before long, Cleo was fast asleep.

She was awakened mid-afternoon by a sudden noise—a loud wailing. Panicked, Cleo darted around to the other side of the tent and hid behind it, peering out to see what was going on.

A boy came out of the back door of the house, carrying a plate. He wasn't the one making the noise— that seemed to be coming from inside. The boy wandered to the end of the yard and sat down on a swing next to the tent. He swung back and forth, nibbling at the sandwich. He was staring vaguely around the yard when he spotted Cleo.

He stopped swinging immediately, and Cleo froze.

The boy slipped off the swing, leaving the sandwich on the grass, and crept toward the tent.

"Here, kitty, kitty…," he called.

Cleo shrunk back behind the tent, just as the wailing started up again.

The boy glanced toward the house. "Is that noise scary? It's just my little brother throwing a tantrum."

Cleo could tell from the boy's voice that he was friendly. And he had another of those sandwiches. Cleo came out a little farther and eyed him hopefully.

"I haven't seen you before," the boy said. "I wonder who has a new kitten. You don't have a collar on, do you?" He looked carefully at the kitten's neck. "Nope, no collar. Hey, where are you going? Oh!" He laughed. The kitten was hurrying over the grass toward his abandoned sandwich. "Do you want it? Oh, wow, you do."

Cleo was already tearing at the corner of the sandwich, gulping it down greedily.

"You're starving!" The boy smiled slowly as he watched the sandwich disappear. "Maybe you're a stray?"

He grinned as the kitten devoured the last bit of sandwich and sniffed the plate all over to see if she'd missed any.

"Who do you belong to? What's your name?" He reached out to tickle Cleo gently behind the ears. "I think you look like a ... umm. Maybe a Smudge? With that dark spot over your eye? But you look like a girl cat to me. Smudge doesn't sound like a girl. What about Patch? Are you named Patch? That's why my mom named our cat Pirate, you know. Because he has an eyepatch."

"Greg! Greg!"

Cleo darted away behind the tent again, and the boy sighed. "There's Mom. I'll come back later with some more food for you. That's if you're still here...."

Chapter Five
A Dangerous Search

Amber followed Sara back into the house, trying to feel hopeful. They had put up posters all along their street and the streets close by. Then they'd gone into the little convenience store at the end of their road and asked if they could put up one on their bulletin board. But it still didn't feel like enough. Amber couldn't just sit in the house, waiting for Cleo to come home. She needed to be doing something.

Maybe she could go and ask some of their neighbors who had sheds and garages if she could check them. Then her eyes widened—she'd just thought of another place where Cleo could have gotten trapped. The family across the street was having a lot of work done on their house and had moved in with their grandparents for a few weeks. Janet, their mom, had told Amber's mom that they'd have to pack everything up in boxes. But that meant some of the rooms were closed up, and there were piles of stuff everywhere— all kinds of places where a kitten could get shut in.

Amber was so excited, and so sure

she was right, that she didn't even stop to ask Mom or Sara to go with her. She'd just have time to catch the builders before they went home, she figured. She slipped back out the front door and crossed the road. Mom would be angry, but if she came back with Cleo, surely Mom wouldn't mind that much…. And Amber was certain she would bring her back.

She hesitated outside number 22, looking for one of the builders to ask. Until now, every time they'd gone past there had been someone around, unloading stuff from vans or hoisting materials up onto the scaffolding. But now there was no one at all.

"Hello?" Amber called, stepping onto the driveway.

No one came. Amber clenched her fists. She just couldn't wait any longer. What if Cleo was starving? She knew it wasn't smart—she'd get into trouble if Mom and Dad found out that she'd gone into Mrs. Williams' yard with all the building work going on. But she had to!

She walked up to the house and tried to peer in through the windows, pressing her nose against the glass. She was trying so hard to see through the dusty panes that she didn't hear one of the builders coming around the side of the house.

"Just what exactly do you think you're doing?"

Amber swung around to find a tall man staring down at her. He was covered in dust. The grayish color made him look like a statue. "I'm—I'm looking for my kitten," she squeaked.

"Your *kitten*?"

"She's missing. I thought she might have gotten shut in...." Amber's voice trailed off—the man looked so angry.

"You shouldn't be here. Don't you realize how dangerous it is to be on a building site?"

Amber hung her head, tears filling her eyes. Then she looked up again, straightening her shoulders. This was too important to let go. "But she's been gone an entire day. What if she's trapped somewhere? Mrs. Williams said that some of the rooms were closed up to keep the dust out—what if she's in one of them?"

"They've all been closed up since we started," the man said, more gently. "And we would have heard her meowing, wouldn't we?"

Amber's head drooped again. "Maybe.... I really thought she had to be here. I'm so worried about her."

"I'll keep an eye out for her," the man told Amber. "What color is she?"

"She's a tortoiseshell, mostly orange, with black patches. We live right over there." Amber pointed across the street.

"All right. I'll let you know if we find her. But now you have to go! What if something had fallen off the scaffolding?"

Amber nodded quickly, her eyes widening. She hurried out of the yard and crossed the street, her cheeks burning. That had been horrible. But at least the builder hadn't insisted on coming back home with her and telling Mom.

Greg slid back through the kitchen, glad that his mom was still occupied with Tony, his little brother. Everyone said that Tony was going through a stage, or that it was the terrible twos, but it basically meant that he was either really, really happy or furious, never anything in between. Right now it meant that Mom wasn't going to notice him sneaking his leftover packed lunch outside to the kitten.

Greg checked—yes, there was quite a bit of his lunch left. He didn't think the kitten would want grapes, but she would definitely be up for cocktail sausages, he decided. Pirate was always trying to snatch them when Mom was making his packed lunch.

He hurried back across the yard,

hoping that the kitten would still be there. *Maybe I should really be hoping that she's gone home*, Greg thought to himself, feeling a bit guilty. The little kitten was probably still not used to being out much.

Then he saw her peeking at him from behind the tent again and forgot to worry about her owner.

As soon as Cleo saw the boy, she darted out from her hiding place at once and came up close to him. Maybe he had more food. She still felt so hungry, even after both those sandwiches. She was used to two good meals and the odd snack of cat treats from Amber. She stopped a short distance away and sniffed at the lunchbox as Greg put it down on the grass.

Greg held out a sausage on the palm of his hand and looked hopefully at the kitten. Then he laughed as the little cat dived at him and started nibbling the sausage right out of his hand. Her mouth was so soft, and her damp nose nuzzled at Greg's fingers.

"You're really nice," he whispered, using his clean hand to pet the kitten's soft back.

The kitten finished off the sausage and looked hopefully into the lunchbox for more. She snagged the last sausage out of the little box and it disappeared in seconds.

"Don't make yourself sick," Greg told

her. "Sorry, that's the last one. There's still a little cheese, though." He took it out and pulled off the wrapper. "There you go." He watched, smiling, as the kitten ate the cheese, too, and then sat down quite heavily and began to wash her ears and face. Her stomach looked a lot rounder than it had 10 minutes ago.

"I wish I knew where you'd come from, Patch," Greg told her. "I probably shouldn't have given you all that food, if you're just going to go home for your dinner. But you looked like you were starving, the way you wolfed down that sandwich."

The kitten licked her bright pink tongue over her nose and then looked at the boy with gleaming golden eyes. She got up and padded a little closer.

Greg gazed down in surprise—he'd thought maybe the kitten would hurry away once the food was all gone. But instead, she clambered onto Greg's lap and flopped down, clearly exhausted by so much eating. She yawned, and then she seemed to melt into the space on Greg's lap, completely saggy, like a beanbag toy. She was asleep.

Chapter Six
Amber's Search Continues

Cleo padded up to the shed and wriggled through a small gap in the boards. She gazed around, hoping to find something else to eat. The boy, Greg, had left her some food there in the morning—toast crusts and the end of a hard-boiled egg. It wasn't like anything Cleo had eaten before, but she'd enjoyed it. She was feeling hungry again now, though.

Greg had shown her this place the evening before. He'd opened the door and gone in to shake the dust and spiderwebs off some cushions from the lawn chairs. He had arranged them into a comfy pile for a bed and filled an old plant saucer from the outside tap with water. He'd even brought Cleo a fish stick. It was a little fluffy from being in his pocket, but she hadn't cared. Then he'd shown Cleo that there was a hole in the shed wall, just big enough for a kitten to squeeze in and out of.

Cleo had spent the night curled up

on the cushions, but she kept startling awake. It wasn't like being in a house. There were strange noises, and they seemed so close with just the thin wooden walls of the shed to protect her. Squeaks and chirps and rustlings in the trees and the flowerbeds, and once, horribly close, a great deep sniff. Cleo had frozen, watching the little hole in the shed wall. After the sniff there had been a pause, a terrifying silence while she'd wondered if the creature was going to claw its way in. But it had gone away, obviously deciding that Cleo wasn't worth the effort. It had left behind a sharp, unmistakable whiff of something wild, and hungry.

She had spent the day exploring the yard—every so often coming up against that smell again. She could still catch a trace of it now....

Cleo hated the thought of spending another night in the shed with that creature so close by. As kind as Greg was, she needed to find her home, where she slept indoors on Amber's bed or occasionally in her basket. She wanted Amber to snuggle up against. She clambered back out of the shed, then crept uncertainly past the house, down the side, and out into Greg's front yard. There she looked out on to the street, wondering how to get home. It was mid-afternoon and quiet, even though there were children's voices in the distance, returning home from school. Cleo peered down the road hopefully, wondering if one of them was Amber, coming to find her. But the voices didn't sound right.

Cleo hopped up onto the wall so she could look around from a high point. The street stretched out in front of her—gray and empty, and completely unfamiliar. Which way should she go?

She sniffed the air, trying to catch a scent of home, but there was nothing. At last she jumped down from the wall and set off down the street, heading for a yard with overgrown bushes spilling out onto the pavement. She would go in short hops, from hiding place to hiding place, she decided. In case that creature was still around.

A strange rattling sound suddenly came around the corner of the road, and Cleo scuttled toward the bushes and ducked underneath. There was a loud clattering and then footsteps. A face appeared under the branches, and Cleo's heart slowed a little. It was the boy who had taken care of her.

"What are you doing?" Greg muttered. "You shouldn't be out on the pavement—I bet you don't understand about cars." He thought of Amber at school, worrying about her kitten getting run over. He should ask her if the kitten had been out in her front yard again. She'd been really quiet at school today, not at all chatty like she usually was.

He scooped Cleo up and snuggled her with one arm, glancing back over his shoulder. His mom hadn't come around the corner yet—Tony was throwing a fit about being in the stroller.

"Don't wriggle too much," Greg warned. "It's tricky riding a scooter with only one hand."

He whooshed the last few feet toward his house and shoved his scooter into the little shed down the side of the yard. The man next door, Luke, had helped Dad build it for all their bikes and things. The kitten was wriggling more and more. "I know," he whispered. "I'm just waiting for Mom to open the door. Here, look!" He slipped his backpack off his shoulders and crouched down, bringing out his lunchbox.

The kitten stopped struggling at once and pricked her ears forward.

"I saved you some of my lunch," Greg told her. "You like cheese, don't you?" He held out a cheese cube to the kitten, who swallowed it almost whole and then tried to burrow into the lunchbox to get more. Greg giggled. "You really do like cheese...." He peered around the corner of the side yard. "Just putting my scooter away, Mom!"

"All right. Close the front door when you come in," his mom called back. "Come on, Tony. We're home now."

"You see," Greg whispered. "Mom's still busy with my brother. She isn't going to notice if I sneak you up to my room, is she? You'll be safe up there, Patch. No more going near the street."

He picked up the lunchbox again, then hurried in through the front door and slipped upstairs.

"Can I make some flyers about Cleo, Mom?" Amber asked as she took off her school shoes. "Mandy suggested it. We could put them through people's doors, in case they didn't see the posters."

"I suppose it could encourage the neighbors to look in their sheds and garages," Mom agreed. "But you're not to go out delivering them without me or Sara," she added with a stern look.

Mom had been really angry the day

before, when Amber had come back in after going to the house across the street. Luckily, Amber hadn't had to explain exactly where she had been—she'd just said that she'd gone out looking for Cleo.

Amber opened up the laptop and started to write the text for the flyer. She dropped in the photograph of Cleo and added a message asking people to check their sheds and garages, then put her mom's cell phone number at the bottom. She printed them out and went into the kitchen to show Mom.

"Do you want to go and deliver them now?" Mom asked. "I have some time before I make dinner."

"Please." Amber hugged her. "I've made enough for our street and

Blackberry Lane. Cleo could have easily gone around into their yards."

Mom nodded and got out her phone. "I'll just text Sara to tell her where we are."

They set off down their street, taking turns to deliver the flyers. It was surprisingly hard to push the flimsy sheets of paper through the slots in the doors, and Amber hoped they wouldn't just get squashed inside and missed.

They were halfway back down the other side of the street when Amber noticed that the builder who'd found her yesterday was coming out of Mrs. Williams' house. She stopped, staring at him in panic. What if he told Mom about yesterday? Mom would be so angry. She delivered the next few flyers extra-slowly, hoping that he'd go back inside before they reached him. But he didn't.

As they approached the house, Amber hid behind Mom. Maybe the builder would think that this was another family looking for their lost cat. But she was pretty sure he knew exactly who she was.

"Hello!" Mom smiled at him. "We're from across the street. Our kitten is missing. Can I give you one of these, just in case you see her? It has my cell phone number on it. She's been gone a couple of days now. Amber here is really missing her."

Amber's eyes widened in panic. Now he was bound to say something....

"Of course," the builder said. "Do you want to hand me a couple more? I can give them to the other guys. I'm Luke, by the way." He smiled at Amber, and she wasn't sure, but she thought he gave her just a hint of a wink, as if to say he'd keep her secret.

Chapter Seven
A Frightening Encounter

"This is my bedroom," Greg explained to the kitten. Then he laughed to himself. "I know you don't really understand a word I say," he muttered. "You're more interested in the cheese than anything else, aren't you? Here...." He grabbed a piece of paper from his desk and used it like a plate for his leftover sandwich.

"I can't keep on giving you sandwiches," he said. "It can't be good for you to be living on my leftovers. But Mom would have seen me if I had gotten you some of Pirate's cat food."

He sat there watching the kitten nibble her way through the sandwich. He hadn't thought about keeping the kitten before. But could he? Of course the kitten might have a home where someone wanted her, even if she didn't have a collar. Some cats just wouldn't wear them. Pirate was an expert at taking them off—

98

or he had been. They used to have to go on collar hunts in the yard, but Pirate didn't go out much anymore. He was fourteen, and his legs hurt. He spent most of his days asleep on someone's bed. Greg really loved him, but Pirate had always seemed more like Mom's cat. He didn't play with Greg that much. Not like this bouncy little kitten…. She could be his very own.

"You've been in my yard an entire day now," Greg pointed out. "At least, I think you have. And you haven't tried to go home. Do you like it better here, Patch?" But that didn't mean the kitten didn't have an owner…. Maybe she was just good at losing collars, too. Greg sighed. She didn't really look like she had been living as a stray for very long. She wasn't skinny or grubby-looking. "I bet someone is looking for you," he admitted. "Well, if you were mine, I'd be making a lot more effort to find you. I think you'll be better off with me."

The kitten gazed around Greg's bedroom with interest and padded over to investigate his bookcase. She gazed up at it, wriggled her bottom a bit, and made a flying leap up to the top. Then she stood there looking proud of herself.

Cleo sniffed at Greg's toy spaceship, and the fur rose a little along her spine. She liked this house, and she liked the boy. But there was something wrong. Cleo hadn't shared a home with another cat since she left the shelter where she'd lived with her mother and the rest of her litter, but she was almost sure there was another cat here. That this house *belonged* to another cat. And maybe the boy belonged to the other cat, too.

She nosed at the spaceship again, leaping back a little as it slid away on its wheels, and the boy leaped to catch it. Then Cleo jumped down again and wandered over to Greg's bed. The other-cat smell was even stronger here. She backed away from the bed, her tail twitching nervously.

Just then the bedroom door swung open, and the boy jumped. "Oh, Pirate, it's only you! I thought it was Mom. Hey, don't be like that...."

A huge black-and-white cat stood in

the doorway, glaring at Cleo. His fat black tail was slowly fluffing up, getting even fatter as every hair stood on end. Pirate hissed, lowering his head to stare Cleo in the eyes.

Cleo felt her own fur rising up, and she hissed, too—a thin, feeble noise compared to the sound the larger cat was making.

"Oh, no," Greg muttered. The kitten was crouched by his bed, looking terrified—but her tail was swishing from side to side in the same angry way that Pirate's was.

"Pirate, she's just a kitten." Greg got up and tried to shoo Pirate out of his room, but Pirate wasn't having any of it. He darted around Greg and jumped at the smaller cat, sending her flying with a big paw.

"No!" Greg yelled, panicking. He'd never expected this to happen. Pirate was so slow and sleepy, but now it was like he was 10 years younger. Pirate was massive compared to the kitten— what if he really hurt the little thing? Greg reached down, trying to grab the kitten. He'd go and put her in the yard and shut Pirate in. But then he jumped back with a yelp. He'd gotten in between Pirate and the kitten, and there were claw marks all down the back of his hand, oozing thin red lines of blood.

Greg looked miserably at Pirate—he'd never seen him look so furious. But he supposed he should have realized. This was Pirate's house, and another cat had suddenly showed up. Pirate was right to be hissing and spitting and clawing. Then he gasped as Pirate launched himself at the kitten, knocking her over with a swipe from his huge paw.

Cleo squealed in fright. This was nothing like the play fights she'd had with her brothers and sisters back at the shelter, and she didn't know what to do. She made a desperate leap, scrambling onto the windowsill.

Pirate sat below, staring up at Cleo, still making those horrible hissing sounds—but he couldn't easily jump to that height anymore.

Cleo didn't know that, though. The window was only open a crack, but she just managed to shoot through the gap before Greg could grab her.

"Come back!" Greg wailed. His bedroom was at the side of the house, and the window looked out on to the two garages—theirs and next door's. The kitten was teetering on the narrow windowsill.

"Come on, here, kitty," Greg called. He was trying to sound calm and coaxing, but his voice was trembling. The kitten hissed at him and jumped down onto the steep, sloping garage roof. She clung to the tiles, her fur all fluffed up and her eyes round with fear.

Greg raced out of his bedroom and almost crashed into his mom in the hallway.

"Greg? What's going on? What was all that noise? Are you teasing Pirate?"

"No! I'll explain in a minute." He dodged past his mom, tore down the stairs, and sprinted out the front door.

"Please come down," Greg whispered, gazing up at the kitten. "I really don't want you to fall."

His mom appeared at the door,

looking really angry. "Greg! What is going on? Get back in here!"

"I can't, Mom. Look…." He pointed up at the kitten, and his mom came over to see.

"Oh!" Mom cried. "Whose kitten is that?"

"I don't know. But she's stuck on the roof." Greg felt bad not explaining how the kitten had gotten onto the roof in the first place, but he hadn't exactly told his mom a lie....

"How on earth are we going to get it down?" Mom said. "Poor little thing— it looks terrified!"

"Kitty!" Tony clambered down the front step and pointed up at the kitten.

Mom caught his hand quickly. "Yes, it is. But the kitty's stuck, Tony. Shh, now, don't scare it."

"Mom, what are we going to do?" Greg whispered.

"Pirate!" His mom gasped, pointing up at Greg's window. "How did he get up there?"

Greg craned his neck to look up at

the window. He could just see Pirate's black-and-white face, pressed up against the opening. But Pirate was too big to squeeze through the way the kitten had. He just stood there, yowling.

Cleo could see him, too. The older cat looked enormous, and she was sure it was about to leap out the window after her. She backed away, hissing, but her claws slipped on the tiles, and she slid even further down the steep roof with a terrified meow.

Mom turned to Greg. "We need a ladder. There's one in the shed—at least, I think there is…. Stay here with Tony and try to calm the kitten down. First I'm going to get Pirate off there before he hurts himself or frightens the little one even more."

She pushed Tony's hand into Greg's and disappeared inside.

Greg looked up at the kitten clinging desperately to the roof and felt so guilty. He never should have brought her into the house.

"Just hold on," he called softly. "It's going to be okay. We'll get you down. And then I promise we'll try and find who you really belong to."

Chapter Eight
Home at Last

"Are you all right?" said a man's voice from behind Greg.

Greg whirled around. It was Luke Bryant from next door. Greg hadn't even heard his van drive up. "Hi!" he said breathlessly. "Do you have a ladder in your van? Mom went to look for one, but she's not sure where it is."

"What do you need a ladder... Oh,

I see." Mr. Bryant peered up at the kitten clinging to the garage roof. "Hold on." He hurried to his van.

Greg went back to whispering nonsense to the kitten and trying to stop Tony from climbing up the drainpipe to get to her. He glanced up at his bedroom. Mom must have grabbed Pirate and put him somewhere safe, because now his window was wide open. Maybe Mom thought the kitten could jump back in. But Greg was pretty sure such a little cat couldn't jump up there from the steep roof, not without sliding back down again.

"I've shut Pirate in the kitchen," said his mom, rushing out. "But I can't find the ladder. I think it must be in the garage."

"It's okay." Greg pointed to Mr. Bryant, who was coming up the path with a tall stepladder. "Mr. Bryant has one."

His mom gave a huge sigh of relief. "Hi, Luke. You showed up at just the right time. I've got a bag of cat treats. I was thinking we could try and coax the kitten back up to the window with them, but it'll definitely be easier this way."

Mr. Bryant unfolded the ladder and slowly moved it toward the garage. "I don't want to scare it away," he said. "Pass me some of those treats, please."

Mom emptied a few into his hand and he climbed up the ladder, holding out the treats toward the kitten. "Come on, kitty. Here, look. Don't you want them?"

Cleo hissed feebly at the strange man. She was so frightened she didn't know what to do—she could only hang on.

Greg watched, his heart thumping. What if Mr. Bryant couldn't reach? Or the kitten tried to dodge him and fell?

"Can you please hold the ladder?" Mr. Bryant called down quietly to Greg's mom. "I need both hands…. Aha! Got you." The kitten wriggled in his arms as he climbed back down the ladder one-handed. "There we are. You're safe now. Yes, you eat those."

He laughed as Cleo sniffed out the cat treats at last, leaning over to nuzzle eagerly at the bag in Greg's mom's hand. "Well, it doesn't look like she's hurt, does it?" He peered at Cleo's black-and-white and orange coat, frowning. "I wonder…. But it's too far, surely. Here, can you hold her a minute?" Mr. Bryant passed the kitten to Greg and dug in his pocket. "Would you say she looks like that?" He held out a piece of paper, with a little picture of a kitten on it.

"Yes," Greg's mom said, looking at the flyer. "I think so...."

"I don't believe it." Mr. Bryant shook his head. "Well, that girl who lives across from the house I'm working on is going to be so happy, if this really is her. Are you Cleo, little one?"

"Cleo!" Greg gasped. He stared at the kitten. "*Amber's* Cleo?"

Mr. Bryant looked thoughtful. "I think her mom did say she was named Amber. She has red hair?"

"That's her! This is Amber's cat? She's in my class. So that's why she's been looking so upset." He looked down at Cleo, his cheeks reddening. He'd wanted to steal Amber's kitten! "But how did she get all the way over here?" he asked suddenly. "Amber told me she lives on the other side of town, by the playground."

Mr. Bryant made a face and nodded toward the van. "Well, guess where that's been parked. Right outside her house."

"Amber did say her kitten was really nosy," Greg said. "She was worried about her getting run over, because she'd started going out into the street."

"You think she got into your van?" Greg's mom asked in surprise, shaking out a few more cat treats and feeding them to Cleo.

"She must have. I'd better take her home," Mr. Bryant sighed. "And apologize for catnapping her."

"You didn't mean to!" Greg's mom laughed. "I'm sure they'll just be delighted to have her back. Do you want to borrow Pirate's cat carrier? The poor kitten probably won't like it much because it'll smell like Pirate, but you'll need to put her in something."

"Before she eats all the cat treats and makes a getaway!" Mr. Bryant agreed.

"Can I come with you?" Greg asked shyly. "I won't get in the way or anything. I'd just like to help take her home."

"If it's okay with your mom," Mr. Bryant said. "You can sit in the front with me and hold the carrier. I don't want it wobbling around."

"Of course you can," Mom said. "Hold on a minute, and I'll get it out of the garage."

Greg smiled. He could imagine how happy Amber was going to be. If he'd lost Pirate, he'd have been so upset.

"Amber, can you get the door?" Mom called. "I've got cake mix all over my hands."

Amber put down the jingly ball she'd found under the shoe rack, blinking away her tears. She kept wanting to cry—everything in the house seemed to remind her of Cleo.

"If it's those window people again, just say no thank you," her mom added.

Amber's mom really didn't like people trying to sell her new windows, and they always showed up when she was cooking dinner. Amber opened the front door, rehearsing a polite go-away smile.

"Oh!" It was the builder from across the street. Amber bit her bottom lip. What if he was coming to tell Mom on her after all? But he was smiling.

"I've brought you a present. My friend and I." He stepped back so that Amber could see the boy next to him, who was holding a plastic cat carrier.

"Greg?" Amber stared at her classmate for a moment—then she looked down at the cat carrier, and her eyes went wide with hope. "Have you…. Have you—?"

"Is it her?" Greg asked anxiously. "We thought it must be."

Cleo scratched crazily at the sides of the carrier, meowing and meowing. Amber was there! The boy had brought her back to Amber! Why wouldn't they let her out?

"Amber, what is it?" Amber's mom came down the hallway, drying her hands on a dishtowel. "Hello, Luke. Is there a problem across the street?"

"Mom, they found Cleo! Thank you so much!" Amber pulled open the latch and reached in to pet the kitten. "I thought you'd never come home...," she whispered, lifting her out and snuggling Cleo against her shoulder. "Where was she?" she asked.

"I found her in my yard," Greg explained. "But I didn't know she was yours. I, um, fed her my leftovers," he admitted. "And then she got stuck on our garage roof, and Mr. Bryant helped to get her down." He couldn't bring himself to tell Amber that he'd lured her kitten into his house and gotten her into a fight with Pirate.

But Amber beamed at him. "Thank you for feeding her. I was so worried that she was going to be starving!"

"I figure she went for a ride in the back of my van," Mr. Bryant added. "I can't see how else she showed up in our neighborhood. It's a good couple of miles away."

"Oh my goodness," Amber's mom said. "She stowed away! I'll have to call

Sara and Dad, and tell them. You don't know how relieved they'll be. We were imagining the worst things...."

"I'm glad I found her," Greg said to Amber.

"Not as glad as I am," Amber said, giggling as Cleo licked her chin. "Thank you so much for bringing her home!"

"You know a lot about cats," Amber said admiringly, watching Greg tickle Cleo on just the right spot behind her ear. She'd invited Greg over to play after school to say thank you—and to let him see how Cleo was. He'd asked Amber about her at school a few times, and she thought Greg must have really liked the kitten.

"Our cat is named Pirate, because he looks like he has an eye patch. He's my mom's, actually. She got him before I was born."

"So he's pretty old, then?"

"Uh-huh. He's pretty slow now—he doesn't race around like this one does. But he's still special," Greg added firmly.

It was true. Pirate might be slow and not that good at chasing toys, but he almost always slept on Greg's feet at night. Mom had told him the other night that Pirate had done that since Greg was a baby. She and Dad had tried to keep him away because they were worried that Pirate might hurt him by accident. But Pirate wouldn't be shooed away—and he was the best one for stopping baby Greg from crying. "In the end we gave up," his mom had said, smiling down at Pirate, who was sitting between them. "He'd obviously decided you were his."

Greg watched Cleo clamber up into Amber's lap and flop down, purring. He petted her ears, and nodded to himself. Amber was Cleo's, and he belonged to Pirate—and that was exactly the way it should be.

HOLLY WEBB

Holly Webb started out as a children's book editor, and wrote her first series for the publisher she worked for. She has been writing ever since, with more than 100 books to her name. Holly lives in England with her husband, three young sons, and several cats who are always nosing around when she is trying to type on her laptop.

For more information
about Holly Webb visit:

www.holly-webb.com
www.tigertalesbooks.com